# ·LIONEL·
# IN THE FALL

# ·LIONEL·
# IN THE FALL

by Stephen Krensky
pictures by Susanna Natti

Dial Books for Young Readers / *New York*

*For Andrew*
S. K.

*To Max and Bea*
S. N.

Published by Dial Books for Young Readers
A Division of Penguin Books USA Inc.
2 Park Avenue
New York, New York 10016

Published simultaneously in Canada by
Fitzhenry & Whiteside Limited, Toronto

Printed in Hong Kong by South China Printing Co.
The Dial Easy-to-Read logo is a registered trademark of
Dial Books for Young Readers,
a division of Penguin Books USA Inc., ® TM, 1,162,718.

Library of Congress Cataloging in Publication Data
Krensky, Stephen. Lionel in the fall.
*Summary:* For Lionel, fall means starting a new school year,
raking leaves, and getting to dress up as a knight and
chase a dragon from house to house on Halloween.
[1. Autumn—Fiction. 2. Halloween—Fiction.]
I. Natti, Susanna, ill. II. Title
PZ7.K883Lk 1987 [E] 86-32876
E

First Hardcover Printing 1987
ISBN 0-8037-0384-8 (tr.)
ISBN 0-8037-0385-6 (lib. bdg.)
3 5 7 9 10 8 6 4 2

First Trade Paperback Printing 1989
ISBN 0-8037-0683-9 (ppr.)
1 3 5 7 9 10 8 6 4 2

The full-color artwork was prepared using pencil,
colored pencils, and watercolor washes.
It was then color-separated and reproduced as
red, blue, yellow, and black halftones.

Reading Level 2.0

# CONTENTS

# BACK TO SCHOOL

Lionel was getting dressed
for the first day of school.
He put on his new shirt
with the stiff buttons.
He pulled on his new pants.
He tied his new shoes tight.
Then he went downstairs.

Everyone else was in the kitchen.

Father was making eggs.

Mother was drinking coffee.

His big sister Louise

was eating cereal.

"Have some breakfast," said Father.

Lionel didn't want anything.

He just pushed his egg around.

"What's the matter?"

asked Mother.

"I have a new shirt, new pants,
and new shoes," said Lionel.
"But I am just the same old me.
I don't match my new things."
"That's dumb, Lionel," said Louise.
"Even for you."
Lionel ignored her.

"Everything looks like it matches," said Father.

"Well, maybe we should check," said Mother.

She opened her purse.

"What are you doing?" asked Lionel.

"You'll see," said Mother.

She took out a picture

and a small mirror.

She gave the picture to Lionel.

"Who's that?" asked Mother.

"It's me," said Lionel.

"You took it last year

on the first day of school."

"That was the old you," said Mother.

She held out the mirror.

"This is the new you," she said.

Lionel looked in the mirror.

Then he looked down
at his arms and legs.
"Everything is longer," he said.
"And my face is not so round."
"You're bigger and stronger now,"
said Mother.
"You match your new things perfectly."

Lionel gobbled up his egg.

"Why are you eating so fast?"

asked Father.

"I have to get to school,"

said Lionel.

"The new me doesn't want

to be late."

# THE NEW TEACHER

Lionel knew everyone in his class.

And everyone knew him.

But nobody knew the new teacher.

"Good morning," she said.

"I am Mrs. Banks."

"Good morning, Mrs. Banks,"

said the class.

Mrs. Banks nodded. "It's nice
to meet you all," she said.
"I'd like to know you better.
Please stand up and tell me
a little bit about yourselves."

Jason was first.

He talked about his pet turtle.

His words came out so fast
they all ran together.

Emily was next.

She talked about her last baseball game.

Her voice sounded higher than usual.

"What about you?" said Mrs. Banks.

She was pointing at Lionel.

Lionel scraped his chair back

as he stood up.

"I'm Lionel," he whispered.

His face turned pink.

"Speak up," said Mrs. Banks.

The pink darkened to red.

"I'm Lionel," he whispered again.

Mrs. Banks shook her head.

"You must speak louder," she said.

"We all want to hear you."

Lionel was now red enough to explode.

"I'M LIONEL!" he shouted.

"AND I HATE STANDING UP HERE

TALKING IN FRONT OF EVERYONE!"

Lionel sat down. He bit his lip.

The class was completely still.

Everyone wondered what
the new teacher would do.
Sarah thought Mrs. Banks would
yell back at Lionel.
Jeffrey thought she would
send Lionel to the principal.

But Mrs. Banks didn't yell.

And she didn't send Lionel anywhere.

She only smiled.

"When I was your age, Lionel,"

Mrs. Banks said,

"I hated to stand up and talk too.

I had forgotten that.

Thank you for reminding me."

She passed out paper to the class.

"All of you can write me
about yourselves instead."

Lionel took out his pencil
and began writing.

He had a lot to say.

# RAKING LEAVES

Lionel was raking leaves

in his backyard.

The leaves were red

and yellow and brown.

The ground was covered with them.

Lionel raked and raked and raked.

His arms got sore.

His legs got tired.

Louise came outside wearing a dress.

She was going to a birthday party.

"Keep up the good work, Lionel,"

she said. "Maybe you'll be done

by Thanksgiving."

She kicked up some leaves and left.

Jeffrey passed her on the driveway.

"Hi, Lionel," he said.

Lionel was glad to see him.

Jeffrey was tall.

He was strong.

Jeffrey could be a big help.

"Nice day," said Lionel.

Jeffrey looked at the yard.

"Too bad you have so much to do,"
he said.

"It's worth it," said Lionel.

"I'm building the biggest pile
of leaves in the world."

Jeffrey laughed.

"Really," said Lionel.

"It will be this big," he said.

He opened his arms wide.

"And it will be fun

to jump in when I'm done."

Jeffrey nodded. "Can I jump too?"

"If you want," said Lionel.

"Of course, I have to finish

raking first."

Jeffrey looked around.

"There are a lot of leaves here,"

he said.

"How long will it take you?"

"A long time," said Lionel.

"Maybe weeks."

Jeffrey smiled.

"I don't believe you," he said.

Lionel started raking again.

"Well, it will take a while," he said.

"And I'm working as hard as I can."

Jeffrey wrinkled his nose.

"You would get done faster
if I helped," he said.

"That's true," said Lionel.

"Maybe even today," said Jeffrey.

"Maybe," said Lionel.

"Do you have another rake?"

"In the garage," said Lionel.

Lionel and Jeffrey worked hard
for a long time.

By late afternoon all the leaves
were in one huge pile.

Lionel and Jeffrey jumped in it
lots of times before dark.

# TRICK OR TREAT

It was Halloween night.

Lionel was going out as

a knight in shining armor.

His father was going out as his horse.

Lionel had made the armor with

cardboard and foil.

His horse was covered with

a sheet and a paper bag.

Lionel and his horse
went out into the night.
It was very dark.
The moon was very bright.

Monsters and clowns were running through the neighborhood.

Lionel was not afraid.

He had his armor and his trusty horse to protect him.

At the first house

a man opened the door.

"Trick or treat," said Lionel.

"I am here to fight the dragon."

The man gave Lionel a candy bar.

"A dragon was here a minute ago,"

he said. "Maybe you can catch it."

Lionel hadn't expected this.

Who could this dragon be?

Jeffrey? Sarah? Benjamin?

His horse didn't know.

"But maybe you can find this dragon,"

he said.

Lionel ran across the street.

A woman opened the door.

"Trick or treat," said Lionel.

"I am here to fight the dragon."

The woman gave him a candy bar.

"You just missed it," she said.

"Try next door."

Lionel and his horse
went from house to house.
They passed witches and ghosts
and clowns and robots,
but no dragons.

Lionel looked for dragon prints

in the grass.

He didn't find any.

Once Lionel thought he heard

the dragon growling in the distance.

His horse had heard something too.

"Where are you, dragon?"

shouted Lionel.

The dragon didn't answer.

Lionel finally gave up

and took his horse home.

The dragon was waiting for them
in the living room.
It had large green scales
and wings like a giant bat.
"Grrrrrr," roared the dragon.
"Uh-oh," said his horse.
"I think we found it."

But Lionel knew that roar.

"You!" said Lionel.

"You were the dragon, Louise."

Louise took off her dragon's head.

"Yes," she said.

"And you couldn't catch me all night."

Lionel dropped his bag of candy.

"Well, I'll catch you now,"

he said.

And he chased her all

over the house.